Chimicnangas and Zoloft

Fernanda Coppel

FOUNDED 1830

SAMUELFRENCH.COM
SAMUELFRENCH-LONDON.CO.UK

MUSIC USE NOTE

Licensees are solely responsible for obtaining formal written permission from copyright owners to use copyrighted music in the performance of this play and are strongly cautioned to do so. If no such permission is obtained by the licensee, then the licensee must use only original music that the licensee owns and controls. Licensees are solely responsible and liable for all music clearances and shall indemnify the copyright owners of the play(s) and their licensing agent, Samuel French, against any costs, expenses, losses and liabilities arising from the use of music by licensees. Please contact the appropriate music licensing authority in your territory for the rights to any incidental music.

IMPORTANT BILLING AND CREDIT REQUIREMENTS

If you have obtained performance rights to this title, please refer to your licensing agreement for important billing and credit requirements.

CHIMICHANGAS AND ZOLOFT had its world premiere at the Atlantic Theater Company in New York City on June 3rd, 2012. The performance was directed by Jaime Castañeda, with sets by Lauren Helpern, costumes by Jessica Wegener Shay, lighting by Grant Yeager, and sound by Broken Chord. The Production Stage Manager was Michael Alifanz. The cast was as follows:

PENELOPE LOPEZ............................... Xochitl Romero

JACKIE MARTINEZ .... Carmen Zilles

ALEJANDRO LOPEZ...............................Alfredo Narciso

RICARDO MARTINEZ .... Teddy Cañez

SONIA MARTINEZ .... Zabryna Guevara

PERSONAJES

PENELOPE LOPEZ – 16 years old, Mexican-American, sassy, loves attention

JACKIE MARTINEZ – 15 years old, Mexican-American, tomboy, wise beyond her years

ALEJANDRO LOPEZ – 38 years old, Mexican, very handsome, metrosexual, a bartender

RICARDO MARTINEZ – 45 years old, Mexican, a very successful lawyer, a quiet man, keeps his emotions to himself

SONIA MARTINEZ – 40 years old, Mexican-American, tired, doesn't understand her own pain

TIEMPO

The present

LUGAR

Los Angeles, California

BLOATED

(Lights come up on **SONIA**, *she is 40 years old with circles under her eyes. She packs a duffle bag as she speaks to the audience.)*

(The sound of a fart...)

SONIA. What? *(to audience)* That wasn't me OKAY. *(beat)* What? You think I'm gassy cuz I ate a chimichanga? Huh? Maybe its because, lately, vodka tastes like tap water AND my eyes look like a third world country. OH and smiling, just seems obsolete My heart feels like a metal weight in my chest affecting the gravitational pull of my insides AND voices of people that died seem to ring in my ears. Like an old teacher of mine, who once told me "Sonia, youth is walking down a hallway with hundreds of open doors, and as you get older and time passes doors close and close..." AND fast forward to this morning, I woke up BLOATED after my 40th birthday dinner cuz I went a little loco and had four chimi-fucking-changas. I looked past my panza to see a pair breasts that USED to look ambitious on my chest AND rolled over to a man that has these gross grey HAIRS growing out of his ears, AND fumbled into my closet to find that my daughter gave me a pair of PANTUFLAS for my birthday! FUCKING PANTUFLAS, I'm 40 not 65 damn it. This can't really be how my life turned out, right? If met the 20 year old version of myself NOW I think she would kick me in the Cho Cho, so that I could feel SOMETHING, ANYTHING again. I mean, I'm 40 years old, damn it. I want to say that with an excited inflection in my voice, not the poutty tone that mimics my breasts.

(She violently zips the overstuffed duffle.)

AND, I FUCKING hate being bloated. None of my pants fit!

*(**SONIA** carries the bag off stage, another faint fart sound is heard.)*

(Lights out.)

VACATION

(JACKIE and PENELOPE lay out in PENELOPE's backyard. They wear bikinis, PENELOPE's is two sizes too small, and sip root beer in the brown glass bottles that look like beer bottles.)

JACKIE. *(mid conversation)...* so basically that's some bullshit.

PENELOPE. Dude, no.

JACKIE. Dude, yes.

PENELOPE. Ugh, dude, I thought it was really good pot.

JACKIE. No, That's like way unacceptable. How long have we been getting high Penelope?

PENELOPE. Uh, forgot.

JACKIE. Since freshman year, Marco's pool party? When Titi shot gunned you and you asked me if that meant that you were gay.

PENELOPE. Oh ya huh, that was a while ago.

JACKIE. Exactly, so you should know the difference between GOOD weed and some CRAP.

PENELOPE. Look, it was dark and my dad called me the second I picked it up. I just got a little nervous.

JACKIE. Ya sure, then you wake up and realize that you have a thing for John, so you won't say shit when he tries to scam you.

PENELOPE. Shut up.

JACKIE. ...*(a moment)* did you hook up with him?

PENELOPE. *(giggles)*

JACKIE. SLUUUUUT.

PENELOPE. Dude I really like him, I mean I know he trembles a lot and he's super paranoid all the time. But when we're alone, I feel like a serious connection.

JACKIE. I HOPE he bagged it.

PENELOPE. What's your problem?

JACKIE. What's your's?

PENELOPE. Psh, your's.

JACKIE. Ugh, your's...you hoochie.

PENELOPE. Fuck you.

JACKIE. I can't I'm not a skinny drug dealer.

PENELOPE. SHHH. *(points towards the window of her house)* Somebody has CIA ears.

JACKIE. Wait, so how was it?

PENELOPE. *(checks to see if her dad was around)* How was what?

JACKIE. The sookie sookie, with the junkie monkey.

PENELOPE. He's not a junkie.

JACKIE. It must have been sick, if you're defending him.

PENELOPE. It was fine.

JACKIE. Fine?

PENELOPE. Yup.

JACKIE. Yup? Yup?
You spend half of my allowance to buy weed that looks worse than my lawn And all you fucking tell me is YUP.

PENELOPE. Yup, thanks for the invite to your pity party but I'm kinda busy now that I have a new boyfriend.

JACKIE. WHAT? You're with our pot dealer????

PENELOPE. *(Loud whisper)* OH MY GOD, Jackie do you not understand that my Dad is home. Shut the fuck up already.

JACKIE. Just tell me one thing...

PENELOPE. No.

JACKIE.	PENELOPE.
You don't /even know	Don't be gross.

JACKIE. Dude, don't be immature.

PENELOPE. HA, I'm the one that's older bitch.

JACKIE. We need a be down for each other, especially now that shit's starting to get hairy.

PENELOPE. Ew, dude. Why you trying to talk about pubes right now?

JACKIE. Quit playing, this is serious shit right here.

PENELOPE. Okay well, I did have a question about something.

JACKIE. Something about sex?

PENELOPE. Well, ya.

I kinda feel weird talking to my Dad about it cuz he's a dude. God, I just really miss your Mom. I mean she's so easy to talk to about everything.

JACKIE. Well my mom's not around right now.

PENELOPE. Ya, dude, I noticed.

I mean, don't you hate it when my Dad drives the carpool? He plays Juan Gabriel all loud. It's REALLY embarrassing.

JACKIE. Word.

PENELOPE. I miss your Mom a lot.

JACKIE. So do I, dude.

PENELOPE. I mean, who am I supposed to talk to around here?

JACKIE. Uh, you have me.

PENELOPE. But you've never had sex.

JACKIE. Ya so, I know the gist.

PENELOPE. Well it was...when his THING.

JACKIE. Penis?

PENELOPE. Ya, THAT. When it was uhhhhh/

JACKIE. Erected?

PENELOPE. Ya, ya THAT.

Well, when he came it was... *(physically eludes to John ejaculating inside of her without a condom)* ...Damn, this is awkward.

JACKIE. It doesn't have to be. How about, THIS I'll ask you questions, then you talk about it.

PENELOPE. Ya, okay that might work.

JACKIE. Great, okay. First question: Did you go?

PENELOPE. Go where?

JACKIE. You know, go...like on the oh, oh, oh tip.

PENELOPE. Sorta, I mean, it was just…probably the most intense five minutes of my life.

Some of it was awkward, and I felt worried about My body even though it was dark in the back of his Civic… But some of it was super passionate and could have been an orgasm/

JACKIE. I don't think you had one.

PENELOPE. Why?

JACKIE. Cuz you would have totally felt it.

PENELOPE. I felt a lot of stuff, I mean John is really sensual and kind when we do it.

JACKIE. Ya, whatever. Sensual and kind doesn't get you OFF.

PENELOPE. Psh, you haven't had one either. Have you?

JACKIE. HELL YES, I have.

PENELOPE. HAVE NOT, with who?

JACKIE. *(refers to her hand)* Manuela.

PENELOPE. You're such a lesbian.

JACKIE. I prefer the term, vaga-tarian.

PENELOPE. Try virgin LEZ.

JACKIE. YA SO, better a member of the V club than have some skinny white boy with a twitch grinding me!

PENELOPE. He's not that bad, dude. He has a steady income and really strong ambitions.

JACKIE. To be the next Eminem?

PENELOPE. You're just being a hater.

The way I see it, this is totally gonna benefit you. I mean, since you're my best friend And I'm with John were gonna get free weed all the time AND his brother is a bouncer at Dakota.

AND John said that if we wear slutty clothes we can even get in on a weekend night.

JACKIE. NO WAY.

PENELOPE. WAY.

JACKIE.	**PENELOPE.**
EEE!!!	EEEE!!!

(**ALEJANDRO** *enters. He carries a tray of nachos and snacks for the girls.*)

ALEJANDRO. I brought your fav.

JACKIE. PB and J?

ALEJANDRO. No more PB and J for my corazon.
Peanuts give her a rash in the *(whispers and points)* bikini area.

JACKIE. *(points and laughs)* PUBE RASH!

PENELOPE. DAAAD.

ALEJANDRO. This isn't the bathing suit I bought for you Penelope Maria Lopez.

PENELOPE. Ya it is, you just don't 'member.

ALEJANDRO. Uh, Sorry?
I don't think I would approve of your cha-chas hanging out like that.

JACKIE. Hee hee, Mr. Lopez said cha-chas.

ALEJANDRO. Go change Penelope.

PENELOPE. But DAD/

ALEJANDRO. What did I say?

PENELOPE. But Jackie's Dad is coming in a little bit. Can I just change after, PLEASE?

ALEJANDRO. Ricardo's coming?

PENELOPE. Be nice Dad.

ALEJANDRO. I'm always nice.

PENELOPE. Now that Sonia's been away you guys have been acting like bitchy drag queens.

ALEJANDRO. When IS your Mom coming back Jackie?

JACKIE. She's, uh on vacation.

ALEJANDRO. Oh is she? She sure didn't mention anything to me about it. Am I supposed to drive the carpool until she comes back? Its been two weeks in a row and your Dad is always too "busy"…

(**ALEJANDRO** *notices that the girls haven't put their drinks on the coasters.*)

ALEJANDRO. Ay DIOS, you guys are gonna stain the new table…

(**ALEJANDRO** *runs to the kitchen.* **JACKIE** *digs into the nachos as if she hasn't eaten in years.*)

JACKIE. He okay?

PENELOPE. Ya, dude. He just has intense diva moments sometimes.

JACKIE. OH, *(takes a big bite of the nachos)*…but he makes heavenly nachos.

PENELOPE. I know, he buys this aged cheese from Trader Joe's. He is like obsessed with it, but it costs like a million dollars.

(**JACKIE** *stares off into space.*)

JACKIE. *(mumbles)* Maybe she didn't like the pantuflas…

PENELOPE. What? What's your issue dude?

JACKIE. Shit is weird at my house.

PENELOPE. Word? Your Dad is probably going crazy with your Mom out of town.

JACKIE. No.

PENELOPE. No?

JACKIE. Nope, I've never seen him happier. I mean, they fight all the time.

PENELOPE. I thought they were gonna see a therapist.

JACKIE. No, my Dad sent my Mom to the therapist cuz she's always emo.

PENELOPE. Like someone else I know…

JACKIE. Shut up! I'm not like my Mom, okay?

PENELOPE. Maybe a little.

JACKIE. Am not, dude. My Mom gets like slit your wrist emo.

PENELOPE. Ya but she would never do that, right?

JACKIE. …right.

PENELOPE. I mean your Mom is so dope, why would she ever try to hurt herself.

JACKIE. I don't know, dude. Sometimes people just do that shit.

PENELOPE. But not Sonia, why would she?

JACKIE. Don't you think it's weird that my Dad isn't really talking about it?

PENELOPE. Maybe he doesn't wanna worry you.

JACKIE. Dude, I don't know. All he does is buy me shit, the other day he just gave me an iphone just cuz.

PENELOPE. Siiiiiiiiick.

JACKIE. Or is it?
Is it that "sick" to work all the time and then plop an Iphone on your kid's bed when her Mom leaves for two weeks without explanation…

PENELOPE. What color iphone is it?

JACKIE. DUDE. I'm worried she's not okay.

PENELOPE. *(pats JACKIE on the back)* Dude, Sonia's fine. She probably just needed a vacation/

(ALEJANDRO comes back out with watering can, a big straw gardeners hat, and a fist full of coasters.)

(He meticulously places the coasters under each of their drinks.)

ALEJANDRO. *(notices tension)* Everything okay here?

PENELOPE. Ya, shit's good.

ALEJANDRO. Speak like a lady, Penelope.

PENELOPE. *(in a British accent)* Everything is fan-bloody-tastic, father.

ALEJANDRO. You don't have to sound like Mary Poppins.

JACKIE. I kinda like it, it's like totally Euro trashy.

ALEJANDRO. I give up.

(ALEJANDRO puts the coaster under JACKIE and PENELOPE's cups. He begins to water plants in his garden. JACKIE watches as she scarfs down more nachos.)

JACKIE. Your Dad loves gardening.

PENELOPE. Ya so?

JACKIE. It's kinda cute. My mom hates doing stuff around the house.

PENELOPE. He has to do it and LIKE it.

JACKIE. Why's that?

PENELOPE. Ugh, cuz I don't have a Mom, stupid. What the fuck is your point?

JACKIE. ...sorry.

PENELOPE. Sometimes you just talk and don't think about what's coming out, Jackie. It's super lame.

JACKIE. I said SORRY.

PENELOPE. I don't wanna talk about IT.

JACKIE. You never do.

PENELOPE. Ugh, your dumb dude... I think your Dad just pulled into the drive way...

(JACKIE *continues to stare at* ALEJANDRO *as he meticulously gardens.* RICARDO *enters.*)

JACKIE. Dang, you're early?

RICARDO. Ya, well this carpool arrangement is exhausting. I don't know how your Mom does it. I had to cancel a couple of meetings to/ pick you up.

PENELOPE. Hi Mr. Martinez.

(RICARDO *looks at* PENELOPE's *breasts, which are busting out of her bikini.*)

RICARDO. Hey? Penelope, you've...you're looking...mature there.

PENELOPE. Well I did just turn 16.

RICARDO. *(looks up trying to avoid her breasts)* Must be THAT. You still have the glow going on, there...uh Jackie, time to get going.

JACKIE. BUT Dad, we were just gonna start doing our Biology homework.

RICARDO. It's World Cup season, honey. US versus Mexico, so hurry up.

JACKIE. But DAD don't you want to say hi to Penelope's dad?

(RICARDO hesitates to look at ALEJANDRO, his caramel muscles glisten angelically in the sun.)

(ALEJANDRO becomes self conscious and puts his shirt back on as he greats RICARDO.)

ALEJANDRO. Hola Ricardo, como estas?

(They shake hands.)

RICARDO. Hi Alejandro, the garden's looking great, as usual.

(RICARDO's squeeze is a little too firm.)

ALEJANDRO. Yup, best of the block every year. Gonna keep it that way/

(ALEJANDRO pulls his hand back towards himself. His hand hurts but he plays it off well.)

RICARDO. Sorry, didn't mean to overpower you there.

ALEJANDRO. No, *(laugh arrogantly)* please. I've been hitting the gym five times a week lately, couldn't be in better shape.

RICARDO. Yes, well being a bartender must allow you a lot of free time to enjoy the pleasures of life.

ALEJANDRO. And being a lawyer is the most redeeming job there is right?

JACKIE. Uhhhhh/

PENELOPE. Dad I think Mr. Martinez was in a hurry to leave, so/

ALEJANDRO. Oh how rude of me, I didn't even offer you a drink or anything.

RICARDO. Well, it is a warm day.
That would have been the first thing I offered if this was my home.

(ALEJANDRO pours RICARDO some fruit drink leftovers from the pitcher he brought the girls earlier.)

ALEJANDRO. But it isn't your home.

(**ALEJANDRO** *shoves the drink into* **RICARDO**'s *face, some spills onto his shirt.*)

RICARDO. Damn it.

PENELOPE. Dad what the hell?/

RICARDO. This is a new Armani shirt.

ALEJANDRO. Sorry, look buy a new one. You can afford it right?

PENELOPE. UH, rude.

(**RICARDO** *tries to wipe his shirt.*)

JACKIE. Dad what about the game? Should we go now?/

PENELOPE. DAD, lend him one of your shirts or something.

(**ALEJANDRO** *hands* **RICARDO** *a napkin.*)

ALEJANDRO. Look come inside, I'll wash the shirt and put it in the dryer.

RICARDO. ...(*still pissed about the shirt*)...

ALEJANDRO. You can catch the first half of the game while I wash the shirt, alright? I insist.

RICARDO. I guess.

(**RICARDO** *and* **ALEJANDRO** *walk into the house together.*)

(*The second they are offstage,* **JACKIE** *and* **PENELOPE** *look to each other.*)

PENELOPE. DUDE.

JACKIE. Our Dads are about to throw down like on some WWF shit.

PENELOPE. I KNOW. Is your Mom coming back from vacation anytime soon?

JACKIE. I think she's out for a minute dude.

PENELOPE. But she's coming back right?

(*Lights out.*)

ZUCHINNI

(**SONIA** *is in the midst of her daily medication routine.*
She sits in front of a bottle of Zoloft pills and a tall glass
of water.)

SONIA. The first time I took anti depressants, I felt so...
defeated? Is that the right word? There I was, this
woman with wrinkles on my knuckles and thick veins
infesting the back of my hands, like my mothers. Pesky
grey hairs on my head and memory slipping from my
brain like water running through my finger tips. Here
I was this GROWN woman sitting calmly at the kitchen
table with a tall glass of water and a small green pill
grinning up at me from the table. Zoloft is like pot,
seriously, its green and makes your eyes squinty from
mass stimulation, your heart delirious and your
stomach opinionated. I wondered if my shrink had
ever taken Zoloft, or smoked weed or felt the type of
thick depression that chronically fogged up my life. I
must have sat there for a good hour, just staring at
that pill and thinking about my mother, the way her
eyes were always swollen as if she had always been
crying. My last thought was Ricardo, well the sound
he makes when he is frustrated with my moods. Its an
interesting mix between a scoff and a gargle from his
throat. Like an "URGGGGHH", I've been putting up
with your bullshit for 16 years bitch "uggggggh". I took
that stupid little green pill and shoved it down my throat
like it was zuchinni, and I HATE zucchini but I read on
the internet that is really good for your eyes. And well,
I want to be able to see better. Just see, especially what's
right in front of me.

(*Lights out.*)

TAEBO TAPES

(ALEJANDRO's living room. ALEJANDRO and RICARDO (has his shirt off) sit awkwardly on a swanky couch. The TV is on, RICARDO sips a drink with a pink umbrella in it. ALEJANDRO taps his finger on the couch, and often looks to RICARDO who is completely focused on the World Cup game.)

ALEJANDRO. Who are you rooting for?

RICARDO. Mexico.

ALEJANDRO. Interesting.

RICARDO. Oh ya?

ALEJANDRO. No, it's just really quiet and I'm bored.

RICARDO. I really love the World Cup, ya know?

ALEJANDRO. I know the feeling, I LOOOOOVE soccer.

RICARDO. Oh ya?

ALEJANDRO. No, I'm kidding. I hate sports.

RICARDO. You're a funny guy.

ALEJANDRO. I am. I find that humor deflects any sort of genuine intention

(Mexico scores! RICARDO, who is half paying attention to the game, and half to ALEJANDRO is now immersed in the game.)

RICARDO. Iralos. Iralos. PINCHE CHICHARITO! *(to ALEJANDRO)* Did you see that? That was amazing!

ALEJANDRO. I could tell by your, enthusiasm.

RICARDO. Do you know anything about soccer?

ALEJANDRO. Kick the ball into the goal.

RICARDO. Right, but there's a logic, a spiritual quest of sorts.

ALEJANDRO. Spiritual quest?

RICARDO. Yes, soccer is so intense.

So physically and mentally demanding. The stamina it takes is, like other worldly *(The game picks up again.)* IRALOS! IRALOS! CHINGASUMADRE!!

ALEJANDRO. Oh my god, I'm gonna get back to watering the plants.

RICARDO. Go ahead. I could use some time alone after the day I've had.

ALEJANDRO. Oh, And I haven't had a long day?? I've been driving the carpool for two weeks in a row. Sonia didn't even give me warning or anything.

RICARDO. I just want a moment of peace and sports, alright?

ALEJANDRO. Ya, okay.
How about you drive the carpool for a week and see how that messes up your whole schedule. Huh?

RICARDO. I can't take them in the mornings. I work. It's hard enough to pick her up after school.

ALEJANDRO. Oh and I don't work?

RICARDO. At night/

ALEJANDRO. My job isn't as distinguished as yours so I might as well be your kid's nanny right?

RICARDO. No, no. That's not what I meant, okay?

(awkward silence)

ALEJANDRO. Do you want another smoothie?

RICARDO. I'm okay, thanks.

ALEJANDRO. I can get you some chips and salsa if you want.

RICARDO. No, I'm good. I had a big lunch.

ALEJANDRO. I make amazing nachos if you're still hungry.

RICARDO. Do you over feed all of your guests?

ALEJANDRO. OH damn it.

RICARDO. I was kidding, Nachos sound alright.

ALEJANDRO. No I just realized something about myself/

RICARDO. I wasn't trying to insult you Alejandro/

ALEJANDRO. No, its just that I saw myself in that moment… and I, um… I'm turning into my mother.

RICARDO. I see, how do you feel about that.

ALEJANDRO. Are you gonna try and be my therapist now?

RICARDO. Nope, just a friend.

ALEJANDRO. That will take some time.

RICARDO. I can wait.

ALEJANDRO. I just don't have a lot of friends. I'm a good parent.

RICARDO. Meaning?

ALEJANDRO. When you're dedicated to being a parent you don't have a lot of free time.

RICARDO. So you don't have a life?

ALEJANDRO. My life IS that girl. This family is my dream.

RICARDO. That's a lot of pressure.

ALEJANDRO. We have each other, and I think we do fine.

RICARDO. I'm sure you do, its just not healthy.

ALEJANDRO. And what is your parenting philosophy?

RICARDO. Let them figure it out, be there as a reference guide.

ALEJANDRO. So you just let Jackie live and wait for her to fall/

RICARDO. Well not fall, no.

ALEJANDRO. Yes, you wait for her to fuck up then you clean it up?

RICARDO. When you put it that way it sounds/

ALEJANDRO. Lazy?

RICARDO. There you go being funny again.

ALEJANDRO. Where did Sonia go, Ricardo?

(**RICARDO** *looks to the television.*)

RICARDO. Red card??? Come on ref, chingado!

ALEJANDRO. Hello?

RICARDO. Hm?

ALEJANDRO. Sonia?

RICARDO. Right, right.

ALEJANDRO. So?

RICARDO. *(points to the T.V.)* The Game.

ALEJANDRO. *(points to the door)* The Plants.

(A moment. Intense eye contact, they quickly look away.)

ALEJANDRO. Penelope…

RICARDO. Jackie…

ALEJANDRO. Right.

RICARDO. Right.

ALEJANDRO. Blah.

RICARDO. Womp.

ALEJANDRO. You can say that again.

RICARDO. Womp. Womp.

ALEJANDRO. When you say it like that.

RICARDO. The sound track to our lives.

ALEJANDRO. That's Great. Just great.

RICARDO. Is it really?

ALEJANDRO. No.

RICARDO. Nope.

(Fireworks!)

*(**ALEJANDRO** and **RICARDO** engage in a passionate kiss. When they pull away their hair is messed up and they are panting.)*

ALEJANDRO. This is crazy.

RICARDO. Just go with it.

ALEJANDRO. Do you think the girls know?

RICARDO. No way, we played it off well.

*(**RICARDO** kisses **ALEJANDRO**, **ALEJANDRO** eventually pulls away.)*

ALEJANDRO. The girls are home.

RICARDO. We can meet at our usual spot later.

ALEJANDRO. What about Sonia? Where is she?

RICARDO. She's not home.

ALEJANDRO. Until when?

RICARDO. What do you care?

ALEJANDRO. She's my friend.

RICARDO. Yes, I know.

(**RICARDO** *looks disappointed and defeated,* **ALEJANDRO** *reaches for his hand.*)

ALEJANDRO. Maybe stay here and Try to be gentle.

RICARDO. I'm always gentle.

ALEJANDRO. Why would I ask you to be gentle, if you're always gentle?

RICARDO. Like this?

(**RICARDO** *kisses down* **ALEJANDRO**'s *neck.*)

RICARDO. Or like that?

(**RICARDO** *continues kissing* **ALEJANDRO**'s *chest.*)

ALEJANDRO. Fuuuuck.

(**ALEJANDRO** *unzips* **RICARDO**'s *pants and reaches inside.*)

(*We hear stomping around and someone trying to open the door to enter the living room,* **ALEJANDRO** *panics and throws* **RICARDO** *off the couch.* **RICARDO** *hits the floor. We hear* **PENELOPE** *from off stage.*)

PENELOPE. Dad? You okay? The door's locked.

ALEJANDRO. Ya everything is, uhhh cumming along?

PENELOPE. Is Mr. Martinez still here?

RICARDO. We're just hangin/

ALEJANDRO. It's half time and we put on the Taebo tapes, sweetie.

PENELOPE. Oh okay…

Hey Dad can me and Jackie go to the mall? We don't have homework and we got a ride there And a ride back.

ALEJANDRO. Sure corazon.

RICARDO. Ya that's fine with me.

PENELOPE. Okay, byeee! XOXO

(*We hear a door slam and someone run off stage.*)

(**ALEJANDRO** *gets up and paces the room.* **RICARDO** *sits back down on the couch.*)

ALEJANDRO. I feel scandalous.

RICARDO. They're.. we have the whole house to ourselves.

ALEJANDRO. We almost got caught.

RICARDO. But we didn't and it's not the first CLOSE CALL.

ALEJANDRO. Maybe it NEEDS to be the last.

(A frustrated **RICARDO** *checks his blackberry* **ALEJANDRO** *re-arranges the pillows on the couch. He needs to fix the pillow behind* **RICARDO**, **RICARDO** *is immersed in his blackberry.)*

ALEJANDRO. Excuse me.

*(***RICARDO*** doesn't move.)*

ALEJANDRO. Excuse me, please?

*(***RICARDO*** doesn't move, he's reading an important email.)*

ALEJANDRO. FUCKING MOVE.

*(***RICARDO*** moves to the other side of the couch.)*

RICARDO. Look, blue balls after a long day isn't fun.

ALEJANDRO. Would you rather they walked in on me giving you head?

RICARDO. But they didn't/

ALEJANDRO. She was right THERE.

RICARDO. Way over THERE.

ALEJANDRO. This is getting annoying.

RICARDO. You didn't think that last night.

ALEJANDRO. There's a lot at stake here in the morning.

RICARDO. Ya, I know.

ALEJANDRO. I don't know what to do.

RICARDO. Be more careful?

ALEJANDRO. We're on the same page about this right?

RICARDO. Psh, ya of course.

ALEJANDRO. This is just sex, awesome-soul-excavating-sex.. right?

RICARDO. Uh, ya. Ya. Of course.

ALEJANDRO. Come here.

(**RICARDO** *walks to* **ALEJANDRO**. **ALEJANDRO**
unbuttons **RICARDO**'s *pants and begins to give him oral
sex.*)

RICARDO. I…love…that…I…I…love…you…love…you…

(Lights out.)

HOMERUN

(**SONIA** *calmly smokes a cigarette and sips on some Vodka as she speaks.*)

SONIA. Do I look like an idiot to you? Come on. I know a thing or two about shit and I KNEW they were fucking. Of course I did. Are you kidding? Sure he was lying to me during the day, but between the sheets, no lie goes unnoticed. And oddly enough, our sex got better after they started fucking. Before, making love to Ricardo was like grad school. Both are a this huge time and soul commitment that JUST provide you with all this equipment. But YOU have to figure out how to get yourself off, all by your lonesome. That's why I dropped out of grad school, I mean, It would drive me crazy how meek Ricardo was. Like he was scared to touch me. Like he was scared of pleasure, like pleasure and pain were synonymous. I had to place him here and there, everywhere, until. One night I found a match box from Alejandro's bar in his jacket pocket. I didn't say anything, it could have been a coincidence. Ricardo has NO LIFE, he gets up Goes to work, comes home and watches sports...that's IT. but THAT night, he came home typsy and horny for once And he fucked me. Guilt and tequila sweat from his back, as I dug my finger tips into him trying to get a hold of what was different. He was fucking me like I was a hole in the ground to rub his dick in. Rough, impersonal, completely dry and I loved it. I loved watching him fuck me, he was doing it so confidently, I felt like his parent, watching him hit his first home run at little league and I was cheering him on, Even though it was hurting me, The ache was so intense that I bit my lip And bled onto the pillow and I loved it. I winced into his soft chest and I loved it. I knew my husband was with another man, and I loved it.

(*Lights out.*)

MALL RATS

(JACKIE, wears jeans, a t-shirt and silver hooped earrings and PENELOPE, wears a tub-top and jeans.)

(They are posted in front of Macy's, JACKIE mad dogs people that walk by. She crosses her arms to her chest and notices that her breast is sore.)

JACKIE. Dude, my boob hurts.

PENELOPE. You on your rag?

JACKIE. Ya so...shouldn't you be on yours?

PENELOPE. *(nervous)* Uh, no. I think we changed cycles.

JACKIE. Oh, weird. *(looks at her breasts)* Hopefully they're growing.

PENELOPE. Awww, you want big boobies. That's cute.

JACKIE. Bitch.

PENELOPE. Small boobies are okay, dude.

JACKIE. Just cuz your boobs grew two sizes in a month doesn't mean you're better than me.

PENELOPE. No, but it means that I'm BALLIN' in the boobie department!

JACKIE. Nah, not it.

PENELOPE. Boobie is a funny word.

JACKIE. Kinda, ya.

PENELOPE. We should make Boobie our new word, like "ohhh snap that shit is boobie!"

JACKIE. Shh, I heard Marta was coming to the mall today. Don't embarrass me.

PENELOPE. Oh really?..who told you.

JACKIE. Lulu.

PENELOPE. Damn, that's a pretty reliable source...*(checks JACKIE out)* and your, uh, wearing THAT?

JACKIE. *(self consciously examines her outfit)* What's wrong with it?

PENELOPE. It's like whatever.

JACKIE. You're like whatever.

PENELOPE. Let's go shopping and give you a lesbian makeover.

JACKIE. What?…no dude, what's your problem.

PENELOPE. Dude, didn't you get the memo? Gay people have excellent taste, so, uh basically you needa step your game up.

JACKIE. I thought that was a gay male stereotype.

PENELOPE. Uh, no? Way to rep the lesbians.

JACKIE. *(self consciously looks around)* Shh… Are you tone def?

PENELOPE. You're pretty Jackie you just, You need a LOOK, something that will make Marta drop her panties and burn them.

JACKIE. I look fine dude.

PENELOPE. DUDE, I'm your best friend. My job is to help you get you laid.

JACKIE. My Mom is my best friend.

PENELOPE. Oh so you blaze and eat flaming hot Cheetos with Sonia after school?

JACKIE. Well no/

PENELOPE. Oh and Sonia helps you run from the Po Po when they roll Lulu's parties?

JACKIE. Not exactly/

PENELOPE. Oh so your mom defends you when all the girls in the locker room make a big stink outta changing in front of you.

JACKIE. Dude/

PENELOPE. Your mom gets made fun of for being your "girlfriend" at school too right? Like guys ask her what your vag tastes like all the time too, huh?

JACKIE. No dude, she doesn't.

PENELOPE. Then stop playing it off. You're like my sister, stupid.

JACKIE. We're tight, dude, no doubt. But that doesn't mean you're always gonna have the answers. You're not always gonna get what the fuck is going on with me.

PENELOPE. Dude I'm trying to be there for you, I mean your Mom freakin peaced out on all of us. We all miss her/

JACKIE. You've never had a Mom, Penelope, how could you miss something you never had.

PENELOPE. Woa. That was messed up.

JACKIE. I'm just saying/

PENELOPE. Dude your Mom is the closest thing I have to a Mom/

JACKIE. Ya, but she's MY Mom. Not your's.

PENELOPE. She's LIKE a Mom to me.

JACKIE. But she's not YOUR MOM. You have your Dad and I have my MOM.

PENELOPE. You have a Dad too.

JACKIE. Dude, he's never around and he barely talks. I wouldn't call him a Dad, I'd call him an Uncle or some shit.

PENELOPE. An uncle that buys you an iPhone son, you better appreciate THAT shit.

JACKIE. I do.

PENELOPE. I would KILL for a MOM and a DAD, so you better rep that shit. You better rep it hard.

JACKIE. Dude, you don't know what my family is like so shut it.

PENELOPE. Um your Mom has driven me to school every morning since kindergarten fool/

JACKIE. The carpool isn't LIFE Penelope.

PENELOPE. I come over for dinner TOO dude.

JACKIE. Ya but you don't hear them fighting after you leave, And you don't find my Dad crying in the garage late at night.

PENELOPE. Maybe he has nightmares?/

JACKIE. And you've never walked in on my Mom all zonked out on Zoloft pills on the couch, like a fucking stoner without the munchies and without the laughter, dude.

PENELOPE. I didn't know she took that stuff dude/

JACKIE. Ya so don't start with your bullshit about how you know everything, Penelope. Let's just go.

(JACKIE *heads for the exit.*)

PENELOPE. Wait. Okay, sorry I have a lot on my mind too…

JACKIE. Like what?

PENELOPE. Well, its kind of a big deal and/

JACKIE. Everything's a big deal to you dude, you're always stealing the fucking show.

PENELOPE. No this time I'm for real/

JACKIE. What are you pregnant or something? *(giggles)* Damn that would be hilarious, I mean your kid would probably smell like a bong…

(PENELOPE *starts to cry.*)

JACKIE. Oh my god. Dude, dude.

PENELOPE. I don't know if I am or not, but I'm late and I'm really scared Jackie…*(sobs)* Dude, what if I'm pregnant? What am I supposed to do? I can't have a kid, I mean what if my boobs get saggy?

(JACKIE *hugs* PENELOPE.)

JACKIE. Maybe it's a false alarm?

PENELOPE. I REALLY wish your Mom was around, dude, like when she left the apocalypse started.

JACKIE. Dude, I'm sorry.

PENELOPE. For what? You can't get me pregnant?

JACKIE. I'm starting to develop a theory about why my Mom left and I just think it's my fault dude.

PENELOPE. Dude, no you're trippin'.

JACKIE. Well I came out to her the night before she left. Maybe she left cuz she's upset that I'm a big hairy lez.

PENELOPE. You haven't heard from her at ALL?

JACKIE. She texts me back sometimes. But never saying where she's at.

PENELOPE. Oh wow.

JACKIE. I know it's pretty hard core.

PENELOPE. NOOO, I just/

JACKIE. WHAT? *(freaking out)* What? Is that baby coming out or something?

PENELOPE. No, no, no I like totally figured it out, dude, we're totally gonna pull a parent trap.

JACKIE. Dude YOU'RE high.

PENELOPE. No actually I'm like a fucking genius

JACKIE. Oh no.

PENELOPE. What?

JACKIE. Whenever you refer to yourself as a genius, I usually end up grounded from your stupid plans!

PENELOPE. Dude, dude no. We're gonna get your parents back together.

JACKIE. How dude, therapy didn't even help them.

PENELOPE. HEY, who scored a 1950 on their SAT pre-test?

JACKIE. …

PENELOPE. Who? I can't hear you…

JACKIE. YOU, you.

PENELOPE. Listen I have a brilliant plan!
It's totally gonna work and then your gonna stop being all emo and go back to normal and then your Mom can help me.

JACKIE. Lay off the drug dealers.

PENELOPE. Check it, your Mom totally answers your texts.

JACKIE. She answers one outta ten a day.

PENELOPE. Cuz your texting her the wrong shit, dude.

JACKIE. I wanna know where she is!

PENELOPE. Dude, your mom is… She's a fugitive, Jackie, she doesn't wanna be found.

JACKIE. But I'm her kid!

PENELOPE. Exactly,

You gotta tell her that you had an emergency. Parents freak out over that shit.

JACKIE. What kinda emergency will get her outta hiding.

PENELOPE. Uhmmmm.

Well either you got shot or…

(*JACKIE and* **PENELOPE** *look at each other for a moment while they think. Bingo.*)

PENELOPE.   **JACKIE.**

Preggers.   Preggers.

(*JACKIE pulls her phone out and begins to text.*)

PENELOPE. AND then she'll come back AND think your straight! Dude, this is the boobie-est idea ever!

JACKIE. No, dude. Didn't work.

PENELOPE. Whatever, just text her that you're at my house and you just took one of those home pregnancy pee-shits…and, and…your really scared and need her NOW. We'll take the bus back.

JACKIE. Shouldn't you be taking one of those? Maybe we should tell your Dad.

PENELOPE. Ew gross no.

A- he would freak out.

B- he wouldn't know what to do.

I'd rather ask your Mom, before I talk to my Dad.

JACKIE. Okay but,

You seriously think she's gonna come out of "hiding", just like that?

PENELOPE. Wanna bet?

(*Lights out.*)

UH OH, SPAGHETTIOS

(ALEJANDRO and RICARDO make out on the couch, both have their shirts off.)

RICARDO. I have an idea.

ALEJANDRO. Your last idea had me sore for days.

RICARDO. Dinner.

ALEJANDRO. What?

RICARDO. Dinner.

(ALEJANDRO keeps kissing RICARDO.)

ALEJANDRO. Oh shit, you must be starving. I can make you a quesadilla.

RICARDO. No, I mean we should have dinner.

ALEJANDRO. Right, I'll go make a quesadilla.

RICARDO. NO, like outside or something.

(ALEJANDRO pushes RICARDO away.)

ALEJANDRO. WHAT?

RICARDO. I know a great Mexican place, serves food as good as my Mom's and/

ALEJANDRO. In public?

RICARDO. It's on the other side of town, they have great caldos and/

ALEJANDRO. So we go have menudo and ignore the fact that you're MARRIED?

RICARDO.	**ALEJANDRO.**
They have /good Carnes too…	I can't do that.

RICARDO. Why?

RICARDO.	**ALEJANDRO.**
You're freaking married/ Like legally bound to someone!	I'm aware of that.

ALEJANDRO. Aren't you paranoid about THIS?
What about your wife, OUR kids, the world???? I mean, Whose supposed to pay for dinner?

RICARDO. What?

ALEJANDRO. There are no rules, there is no logic. There's no, woman in this equation.

RICARDO. Do you want to be with a woman?

ALEJANDRO. Why are you pushing? I told you, I'm dedicated to Penelope. What if she ends up suffering just because I wanted to indulge in good sex.

RICARDO. Is that really all this is to you?

(ALEJANDRO *points to a large bruise/cut on his arm.*)

RICARDO. That's really gross.

ALEJANDRO. You see this? You know how I got this?

RICARDO. You need to put something on that/

ALEJANDRO. I tripped on the stairs outside.

RICARDO. Were you drunk?

ALEJANDRO. No I wasn't.

You had just kissed me goodbye and I got out of the car turned around and fell on my walk up to the door. Can you believe that? I fell walking UP the steps.

RICARDO. So you have bad hand eye coordination?

ALEJANDRO. NO!

…fuck it, look. I do feel things, deeper things than usual. When I kiss you, I can't feel my legs, I have no grounding, no balance, except for your eyes. And, when you're not looking I don't know what to think of it. It feels like nothing, like a silly idea. Like those impulsive voices that tell you to leave your kid and buy a convertible and drive as fast as you can, and as far away from your life as you can. But then the night comes and it's easier to love you in the dark…where no one can SEE us.

RICARDO. You're in love with me.

ALEJANDRO. We have children. We have obligations. We can't LIVE in the fucking dark, Ricardo.

RICARDO. Look, this is getting intense for me/

ALEJANDRO. Seriously? How intense?

RICARDO. Look, I just wanted to grab some dinner/

ALEJANDRO. Bullshit, you just admitted that things are "getting intense". I mean, have you even REALLY thought about it. Feelings aside, just like sorted out the FACTS.

RICARDO. Facts...

ALEJANDRO. FACTS. YES.

Do you think that we're magically gonna just move to West Hollywood together with our two daughters *(that fight like cat and dog as friends)* and be the gay power couple neighbors with an amazing lawn cuz the one that acts like the "girl" has a green thumb. And bleach our fucking teeth and wear those stupid rainbow bracelets, and then adopt some baby from China and march it up and down the street during the PINCHE gay pride parade de MIERDA...and, and just live happily every after?? Without any fucking consequence?? /HUH???

*(**RICARDO**'s cell phone rings, one of those cheesy techno rings that get on people's nerves in public places.)*

RICARDO. I don't have all the answers/ okay?

ALEJANDRO. That isn't OUR/ life.

RICARDO. I'm just following my gut with/ this.

*(**RICARDO**'s cellphone continues to ring.)*

ALEJANDRO. We aren't the kind of people that can afford to do that/

*(Ring, Ring, Ring...**RICARDO** looks at the caller Id and Immediately stands.)*

RICARDO. Sorry, I REALLY have to take this..

*(**ALEJANDRO** tries to block **RICARDO**'s way but **RICARDO** steps over **ALEJANDRO** and nervously paces while talking on the phone.)*

RICARDO. Hey – how's it go/ Ya, she left a couple of hours ago...Why?

*(**ALEJANDRO** looks to **RICARDO**. **RICARDO** waves him away.)*

(We hear the front door open and two people enter.)

RICARDO. I'll take care of this I know what the arrangement was mija/
Sorry it slipped, I know you don't like to be called tha/
This has nothing to do with my parenting abilities..
You stay there, I'll take care of this. I can handle it/

(**PENELOPE** *and* **JACKIE** *prance in excitedly.*)

(**RICARDO** *motions them to have a seat, he looks pissed and continues arguing on the phone.*)

PENELOPE. Hey Dad, what's going on?

ALEJANDRO. I have no idea. How was the mall?

PENELOPE. Fine, there's an awesome sale at Pier One that you should check out/

ALEJANDRO. Oh really?

PENELOPE. Ya, maybe we can finally buy that chair/

RICARDO. You don't have to attack ME because something goes awry/

(**RICARDO** *looks upset, continues to pace while on the phone.*)

JACKIE. Mr. Lopez what's wrong with my Dad?

ALEJANDRO. I don't know honey, I'm as in the closet as you are.

RICARDO. Listen…Calm down/ No, No, NO. Jackie is right in front of me.

JACKIE. Uh oh.

(**JACKIE** *whacks* **PENELOPE**'s *leg.*)

PENELOPE. Ouch.

JACKIE. Good going tard face.

PENELOPE. What dude?

RICARDO. Yes, I'll handle this…
No I'm perfectly capable, yes, just try to relax okay?/
Hello?…Hello?

(RICARDO looks to his cellphone then to ALEJANDRO.)

ALEJANDRO. What was that about?

RICARDO. Ladies do you want to answer that?

PENELOPE. WOW look at the time. I have a TON of homework to do, Ima just uh…

(PENELOPE tries to make a quick escape.)

ALEJANDRO. So enthusiastic about homework all of a sudden?

PENELOPE. You know how I love Trig Dad…

ALEJANDRO. Freeze, turn around.

(PENELOPE sits back down on the couch next to a terrified JACKIE.)

ALEJANDRO. I smell some mierda around here and we're gonna get to the bottom of this. RIGHT now.

JACKIE. Good going.

PENELOPE. Whatever.

RICARDO. My phone call was really disturbing/

PENELOPE. I'm sorry to hear that/

ALEJANDRO. Who called you?

JACKIE. Look Dad, I can explain everything. We really didn't have bad intentions and everything will make sense/

(JACKIE puts her hand on PENELOPE's leg, like a "hello do you have my back here dawg?" PENELOPE puts her hand on JACKIE's and finishes her sentence.)

PENELOPE. Mr. Martinez, we didn't know how else to come out with/

(ALEJANDRO stands up in shock.)

ALEJANDRO. Are you TWO??? Penelope are you a lesbian??!?

PENELOPE. ME?

ALEJANDRO. *(Freaking out)* Oh GOD, Oh GOD, Putita Madre!

(ALEJANDRO *leans into* RICARDO*'s shoulder as* RICARDO *consoles him.*)

ALEJANDRO. This can't be, Dios Mio…

(JACKIE *observes.*)

JACKIE. Since when are you two so close?

(ALEJANDRO *pulls away and slams his hand into the coffee table.*)

RICARDO. We had an intense afternoon, calm down Ale/

(ALEJANDRO *gets up and gets in* PENELOPE*'s face aggressively.*)

ALEJANDRO. Penelope, amor mio. Tell me the TRUTH.

PENELOPE. Breathe Dad/

ALEJANDRO. Do you like panocha hija? DO YOU.

PENELOPE. *(Shocked)* Dad, I/

(JACKIE *grabs* ALEJANDRO *by the shoulders and removes him from* PENELOPE*'s face.*)

JACKIE. Mr. Lopez this is getting out of hand.

(ALEJANDRO *grabs* JACKIE*'s hands off his shoulders and holds onto them as he goes off.*)

ALEJANDRO. Is Jackie your special "friend"?? It makes so much sense, they've been so close for so long. I should have seen it coming… This is my fault, I should have/

(RICARDO *grabs* ALEJANDRO *and sits him down on the couch next too him.*)

RICARDO. Okay, you need to calm down.

ALEJANDRO. Why are you SO calm?

PENELOPE. Cuz you're being schizo.
   Mr. Martinez? Listen me and Jackie are just friends. My Dad has a tendency to freak out.

ALEJANDRO. Don't talk about me like I'm not here.

RICARDO. How about we let THEM talk?

ALEJANDRO. Fine.

(awkward silence)

RICARDO.	**ALEJANDRO.**
…well?	…hello?

PENELOPE. Go ahead, Jackie.

JACKIE. Ugh, it was your "genius" idea.

PENELOPE. Oh whatever I was trying to help you.

JACKIE. HA, like your plan didn't totally benefit YOU/

*(**ALEJANDRO** gets up.)*

ALEJANDRO. Are you a lesbian, Penelope? ANSWER THE FUCKING QUESTION.

*(Everyone is shocked at **ALEJANDRO**'s outburst.)*

PENELOPE. No Dad, I'm not…

*(**ALEJANDRO** lets out a huge sigh of relief and sits. **RICARDO** gives him a dirty look.)*

ALEJANDRO. Thank Jesus in the heaven. God is good, Alleluia!

PENELOPE. Woa what do you have against gay people?

ALEJANDRO. Nothing, as long as they aren't MY daughter. MY daughter will get married to a nice man and have nice children and a nice life.

PENELOPE. Uh, do you feel the same way Mr. Martinez?

RICARDO. Jackie's not gay, she's pregnant according to her mother.

ALEJANDRO. NO WAY!

JACKIE. Not technically.

RICARDO. How can you be technically pregnant?

JACKIE. Well Dad it's complicated/

RICARDO. You sent a text to your Mother saying that you were pregnant and now she is PISSED.

PENELOPE. Pregnant can mean so many things nowadays…

ALEJANDRO. Stop being a smart ass.

RICARDO. Why did you do that Jackie? I want an explanation!

JACKIE. Chill Dad.

RICARDO. DO NOT TELL ME TO CHILL! Just explain!

JACKIE. *(to* **PENELOPE***)* You're such a dumbass.

PENELOPE. I thought it was a good idea.

JACKIE. You always get ME in trouble with your "good ideas"!

ALEJANDRO. Are you in on this?

PENELOPE. Like Jackie said its complicated…so uma Jackie will explain it best…Jackie?

JACKIE. Uh/

RICARDO. Well?/

ALEJANDRO. Jackie?/

RICARDO. Uh, any time here./

ALEJANDRO. The truth please./

RICARDO. *(to* **ALEJANDRO***)* Jackie wouldn't lie/

ALEJANDRO. Neither would Penelo/

RICARDO. She just did/

ALEJANDRO. Oh this is NOT Penelope's fault/

JACKIE. STOP. BOTH of you. Look…

> (**JACKIE** *looks to* **PENELOPE, PENELOPE** *shakes her head wildly.*)

Penelope thinks she's pregnant.

RICARDO.	**ALEJANDRO.**
What?	WHAT?

PENELOPE. UHHH, BITCH.

JACKIE. You're the bitch, all letting me burn at the stake from YOUR "parent trap" bullshit plan.

PENELOPE. Oh ya? Well Jackie's gay!

RICARDO.	**ALEJANDRO.**
WHAT?	What?

RICARDO. Why did you text your Mother saying you thought you were pregnant.

JACKIE. Penelope thought it would make her come home/

ALEJANDRO. Since when have you been having sex?

PENELOPE. I dunno, a month or so?

RICARDO.	**ALEJANDRO.**
Chingado.	Chingado.

JACKIE. Is she coming back? I'm worried about her.

RICARDO. Your Mom needed some time to herself, Jackie.

PENELOPE. But I wanted to ask Sonia about what to do.

ALEJANDRO. Why Sonia?

PENELOPE. I mean, cuz she's a girl and if I had a Mom I'd ask her.

ALEJANDRO. It's up to US to deal with this. And were GOING to deal with it. TOGETHER.

(Lights out.)

MICKEY MOUSE

(**SONIA** *has just hung up the phone with* **RICARDO**. *She plays with a mickey mouse key chain that's connected to her purse.*)

SONIA. Once, I had to get my six year old Jackie to bed. After chasing her around the house and stubbing my toe on Ricardo's damn rocking chair, I finally caught my daughter and carried her to her room. A familiar drill, I stuffed her chubby little panza into some Mickey Mouse PJs and tightly tucked her into a Mickey Mouse bed spread hoping the cotton would warm her spirit and keep the nightmares away. I leaned into her forehead and gave her a kiss perfectly in between both eyes, making her unibrow glisten with my loving saliva. I said my usual, "Que sueñas con los angelitos, mi vida". And Jackie's small hands crept from the under the covers and sweetly wrapped around each side of my face. We gave each other a look that I wish I could frame, of pure and uncensored love. I think she was overwhelmed or maybe figuring out boundaries or what my role is in her life? But Jackie, then pulled my face in and gave ME a kiss. A soft kiss on the lips. I was visibly shocked, I took her hands from my face and told her that it was completely inappropriate. "You don't kiss your mother on the lips, Hija! You just don't. That's what you do to your boyfriend". Jackie's face, like a winter sunset, quickly faded from confused-to-regrettable-to-mortified shrieks of tears. She turned away from me and cried into her pillow, as if it was the first time she experienced unrequited love and I just shredded her tiny, Mickey Mouse worshipping heart. And THEN I started crying! Ya! I mean, it broke my heart that I broke her heart and we just laid cramped in her twin bed crying like two guests on the Oprah Winfrey Show. I feel asleep there, snuggled next to my weepy daughter And the snotty/salty image of that stupid mouse we all know and love.

(*Lights out.*)

VAG IN THE AIR

(Gynecologist office, afternoon, **PENELOPE** *has her legs in stirrups.)*

*(***ALEJANDRO*** knocks before he enters.)*

ALEJANDRO. Honey?

PENELOPE. DAD? Where's the doctor?

ALEJANDRO. He's coming.

PENELOPE. But I've been waiting for-freaking-ever and this place is depressing.

ALEJANDRO. It's Planned Parenthood not Disneyland.

PENELOPE. Ugh.

ALEJANDRO. Are you comfortable?

PENELOPE. No.

ALEJANDRO. Oh, is there something I can get for you?

PENELOPE. Dude, Dad look at me.

*(***ALEJANDRO*** takes a second to take a good look at* **PENELOPE** *'s vulnerable state.)*

PENELOPE. My vag is up in the air for the whole world to see.

ALEJANDRO. Do you want some water or something?

PENELOPE. I WANT to go home.

ALEJANDRO. This is part of being an adult, learning how to deal with the consequences.

PENELOPE. It's not my fault.

ALEJANDRO. Whose fault is it?

PENELOPE. It was an accident.

ALEJANDRO. No, Penelope sex is like buying a motorcycle. Sure it looks cool and shiny but at any turn you could crash into a taco truck and DIE.

PENELOPE. I'm hungry.

ALEJANDRO. Hopefully you're not PREGNANT and we can go home and have a nice long dinner together.

PENELOPE. I wanna eat alone in my room.

ALEJANDRO. I don't care what you want at this point.

PENELOPE. Ya, you do. You always care.

ALEJANDRO. That's gonna change, starting now.

PENELOPE. Whatever.

> *(A moment,* **ALEJANDRO** *nervously paces the room, he grows uncomfortable as he examines the gynecologist's tools.)*

PENELOPE. Why are you acting like you've never been here?

ALEJANDRO. Do I look like I need to see the Gynecologist on a regular basis?

PENELOPE. Didn't you come with my Mom?

ALEJANDRO. No.

PENELOPE. Damn, that's kinda messed up/

ALEJANDRO. Let's not get into that/

PENELOPE. That's what you ALWAYS say when I bring up MOM/

ALEJANDRO. This isn't a good time/

PENELOPE. You always say that too/

ALEJANDRO. Let's play the quiet game, you start.

PENELOPE. I think that's why I used to get those stomach aches.

ALEJANDRO. I thought they went away with the tea I started to make you.

PENELOPE. No, they went away when I met John.

ALEJANDRO. John is?

PENELOPE. My boyfriend.

ALEJANDRO. I didn't know/

PENELOPE. There's a SHIT LOAD you don't know/

ALEJANDRO. But we talk all the time.

PENELOPE. About nothing.

ALEJANDRO. I get tired.

PENELOPE. I get lonely.

ALEJANDRO. What's missing Penelope?
What are you looking for that lead you to have unprotected sex with a, a..

PENELOPE. John?

ALEJANDRO. John, ya.

PENELOPE. He's different.

ALEJANDRO. So you have a deep connection?

PENELOPE. Ya kinda.

ALEJANDRO. And feel comfortable talking about everything?

PENELOPE. Well he's kind of a loner at school, so he's a really good listener.

ALEJANDRO. Why is he a loner?

PENELOPE. He just has, uh, really strong ambitions that don't vibe well with most people.

ALEJANDRO. What does he do?

PENELOPE. He's, um, an organic specialist.

ALEJANDRO. Organic in what sense?

PENELOPE. He deals with green things.

ALEJANDRO. Okay? So he's a gardener.

PENELOPE. Weren't we gonna play the quiet game?

ALEJANDRO. Why don't you have John over?

PENELOPE. It's complicated, he works crazy hours…

ALEJANDRO. I thought gardeners only worked in the mornings?

PENELOPE. He's not a gardener.

ALEJANDRO. Penelope Maria?

PENELOPE. He sells herbal remedies.

ALEJANDRO. Are you dating a shaman??

PENELOPE. He's something, something else/

ALEJANDRO. Does he sell "something else"? Is that why you kept him a secret?

PENELOPE. I don't know what you're talking about.

ALEJANDRO. Oh come on, I know you and Jackie are the mini Cheech and Chong okay?

PENELOPE. I seriously don't know what you're talking about Dad.

ALEJANDRO. Your room smells like Northern California...

(**PENELOPE** *doesn't get it.*)

Ya know, pot territory?

PENELOPE. You never say anything.

ALEJANDRO. I'd rather you smoke weed in your room, than do something stupid like get pregnant...

PENELOPE. I'm not stupid.

ALEJANDRO. You have a secret pot dealing boyfriend that's as fertile as the Miracle Grow I use on the lawn...that's not exactly smart behavior.

PENELOPE. He wasn't a secret.

ALEJANDRO. Why didn't I know about HIM?

PENELOPE. Dad, I, just..

I REALLY feel awkward doing or talking about girl stuff with you.

ALEJANDRO. Oh.

PENELOPE. You wanted to know.

ALEJANDRO. I know I did.

PENELOPE. Is it weird for you?

ALEJANDRO. Yes, well...I think it's weird that you constantly push me away when I'm all you have.

PENELOPE. I have Sonia too.

(*a moment*)

ALEJANDRO. I try really hard.

PENELOPE. I know/

ALEJANDRO. And it's still not good enough. I work over time at a fucking bar, where people call me JOSE, cuz that must be what every Mexican Male is named to come home exhausted, to a dirty house and an adorably little hungry MOUTH, that belongs to this whole BEING that I'm in charge of FOREVER... like even when you get older, Penelope, you'll STILL NEED ME but on this whole other level, SO BASICALLY the only break I get is when you're sleeping or dead. And it all amounts to nothing, what if you're pregnant? I'm gonna feel like a failure.

PENELOPE. You're not.

ALEJANDRO. I'm supposed to protect you.

PENELOPE. You can't protect me from everything.

ALEJANDRO. I can try.

PENELOPE. You can for the 12 hours in the day when I see you but what about the 12 hours of the day where we live separate lives?

ALEJANDRO. Is it because I'm a man?

PENELOPE. DUH DAD.

ALEJANDRO. Other girls are close with their fathers.

PENELOPE. We're pretty close.

ALEJANDRO. Then why are we at the gynecologist taking a pregnancy TEST!?!

PENELOPE. We could have just gone to the drug store and taken one of those home pregnancy pee-shits/

ALEJANDRO. No we couldn't have/

PENELOPE. YES, we could have Dad. Other women do it all the time/

ALEJANDRO. You are not "other women", you are my daughter and I want what's best for you. And being here right now is NOT what I had in MIND.

PENELOPE. Ugh, you don't understand.

ALEJANDRO. I think I see things crystal clear/

PENELOPE. You don't. I wish my Mom was here.

ALEJANDRO. Don't start.

PENELOPE. I wish Sonia was here.

ALEJANDRO. Why Sonia? She JUST drives the fucking carpool.

PENELOPE. She's like a Mom to me. We talk about shit.

ALEJANDRO. But she's NOT your mother.

PENELOPE. Neither are YOU.

ALEJANDRO. Quiet Penelope, I'm warning you.

PENELOPE. Maybe if I had a MOM, I wouldn't fucking be HERE.

*(An enraged **ALEJANDRO** stands just as a strong knock is heard on the door.)*

ALEJANDRO. *(to the door)* Just a second.

*(A beat, **ALEJANDRO** really takes this in.)*

ALEJANDRO. Ya. Maybe, corazon.

Maybe that would have been the case *(to the door)* Come in doctor.

(Lights out.)

STARFUCKS, OOPS, I MEANT STARBUCKS.

(**RICARDO** *and* **JACKIE** *sit at a Starbucks,* **JACKIE** *has finished a Venti sized Frapi Cochinos and is slurping the remains.*)

RICARDO. Can we lower the sound affects?

JACKIE. Sorry.

RICARDO. Why did you do that?

JACKIE. I was enjoying every last taste.

RICARDO. No Jackie, I meant today's fiasco..texting your Mom, preggers, etcetera, etcetera.

JACKIE. I miss her.

RICARDO. You didn't say anything to me about it.

JACKIE. You didn't ask.

RICARDO. I didn't know I had to ask.

JACKIE. Ya Dad, that's generally how conversations are started.

RICARDO. We talk.

JACKIE. We don't.

(**RICARDO** *gets a text and looks to his phone.*)

RICARDO. What are we doing right now, yoga?

JACKIE. This didn't happen on its own. I had to make this huge stink for you to ask me what's up.

(**RICARDO** *sends a text.*)

RICARDO. I'm really busy.

JACKIE. I'm your kid.

RICARDO. I know and I'm trying to make a better life for you. That's why I'm so busy!

JACKIE. Maybe I don't want a "better life".

RICARDO. You don't know what you want, you're 15.

JACKIE. I do.

RICARDO. When I was your age I wanted to be a ninja/

JACKIE. I want you.

RICARDO. You have me.

JACKIE. Nobody has you Dad, not even Mom.

RICARDO. That's not true.

JACKIE. You're like sand or something.

RICARDO. *(laughs)* Excuse me?

JACKIE. Ya, like sand. You heard me.

RICARDO. I don't understand.

JACKIE. You make everyone feel like they can get a hold of you, but like sand you fall between the cracks of fingers and shit.

RICARDO. Woa. When did you get so deep?

JACKIE. I'm a sensitive person.

RICARDO. Like your mother.

JACKIE. Where is she?

RICARDO. She needed to get away.

JACKIE. Are you getting a divorce?

RICARDO. No, Jackie. I don't think we are.

JACKIE. You don't "think"? Do you even know where she is?

RICARDO. I do.

JACKIE. Why don't you go to her and bring her flowers and tell her you love her and you want her back?

RICARDO. She doesn't want me too.

JACKIE. How do you know?

RICARDO. I just do.

JACKIE. Do you love her?

RICARDO. Love is complicated/

JACKIE. That's a cop out. Don't give me cop outs Dad or I'll text Mom and say your having an affair or some shit! That will make her come back then you'll have to deal with it.

RICARDO. Now, Now, let's stay calm please!

JACKIE. I want answers.

RICARDO. Answers don't always add up to peace.

JACKIE.	RICARDO.
Ya they do.	Shh, Jackie.
And I want them	
I want them NOW, Dad.	
I want / ANSWERS.	

(RICARDO looks around Starbucks making sure that JACKIE isn't making a scene.)

RICARDO. Shh, I'm convinced that... Sexuality is the cruelest thing God ever invented, OKAY? It's like she/ he was bored one day and created all these Beautiful people out of dust or clay or something, and THAT wasn't good enough..he played with them for a while and got really bored, real quickly because they were too perfect... So he gave them hearts and he gave them passions and he basically created her/his own soap-opera world to watch while he/she sits on a couch in the sky eating pretzels, drinking cheap beer, and scratching his balls or vagina and laughing at the stupid people that don't know what they FUCKING WANT!

(A moment, JACKIE is puzzled. RICARDO pants after his rant, he doesn't do this often.)

JACKIE. What does sexuality have to do with Mom?

RICARDO. Nothing, I have things on my mind.

JACKIE. Did she leave because of me?

RICARDO. Now way, your mother loves you.

JACKIE. I came out to her the night before she left.

RICARDO. Really?

JACKIE. Ya...she didn't tell you?? Do you talk to anyone? JEEZ.

RICARDO. No, not really.

JACKIE. How does that work?

RICARDO. I'm not supposed to talk.

JACKIE. Why do you have a mouth?

RICARDO. For eating so that I can, ya know, sustain my body and/

JACKIE. You're clueless.

RICARDO. No, actually I'm a pretty smart guy.

JACKIE. If you're so smart why are you in this mess?

RICARDO. *(stumped)*…

JACKIE. Hm, might wanna get your money back from those fancy schools Dad.

RICARDO. How do you know?

JACKIE. Cuz you have no problem solving skills, you can just quote a bunch of dead people.

RICARDO. No, I mean that you're gay.

JACKIE. Oh.

RICARDO. Have you slept with men?

JACKIE. No.

RICARDO. But you've slept with women?

JACKIE. No.

RICARDO. Jackie, how do you know what you like if you don't try it? Maybe you don't really know.

JACKIE. I know.

RICARDO. HOW?

JACKIE. It's complicated/

RICARDO. Oh, see you don't know how to talk either!

JACKIE. I do a better job than you do.

RICARDO. Doubt it.

JACKIE. *(mumbles)* Janet Jackson.

RICARDO. What was that?

JACKIE. Janet Jackson.

RICARDO. The singer?

JACKIE. She's not just a singer, she's a pop icon.

RICARDO. What about her?

JACKIE. I just know cuz of her.

RICARDO. That makes no sense.

JACKIE. It never does.

RICARDO. *(laughs)* You know you're gay because of a singer? Did you fuck her or something? *(snorts and continues laughing)*

JACKIE. NO, shit. You're fucking ignorant.

RICARDO. Hey, don't talk to me like that.

JACKIE. I just...I love her music...and...um Have you ever seen Poetic Justice?

RICARDO. No.

JACKIE. Ya know that movie where Janet is this emo poet lady who falls in love with Tupac, whose a mailman. That was the first time, I...just...saw her...and..well...I drenched my underwear.

RICARDO. You peed yourself?

JACKIE. No, not that. It was...

Not like your average wet feeling, it was like a water balloon had popped in my fuckin vag and, I HAD to leave the room.

RICARDO. Ew Jackie! That's gross.

JACKIE. Grow up Dad.

I was sooooo embarrassed, I told Mom I just had to pee really bad, and ran into the bathroom but in actuality I was hot...I was hot, for Janet. I didn't want Mom to worry so I quickly changed and ran back in to watch the movie. But then that "Again" song came on and she was all like "I'll never fall in love with you again", and talking about her soul and shit, and crying out *(sings)* "Hold ME, HOLD ME". I melted like some grilled cheese! I just, melted and I knew that the tingling in my chest was something that wouldn't go away. No matter how much I pretended like it was nothing. This was who I am, and this is what makes me tingle *(shrugs)* That's the way love goes.

RICARDO. Okay?

JACKIE. You wanted to know.

RICARDO. So Janet made you aroused? And that makes you a lesbian for life?

JACKIE. I don't know Dad, I'm not an expert.

RICARDO. But you're gay.

JACKIE. Yes, is that a problem for you?

RICARDO. I don't think so.

JACKIE. Is it a problem for Mom?

RICARDO. I don't know.

JACKIE. Why did she LEAVE?

RICARDO. Her therapist said she needed time away.

JACKIE. But why? Is she gonna do THAT again?

RICARDO. No, it's different this time.

JACKIE. How do you know for sure?

RICARDO. I just do.

JACKIE. What if we find her zonked out next to vodka and some pills again, and then she has to spend time in the hospital again.

RICARDO. This time she was specific. She just told me where to pick her up and gave me a date to do it, and told me to leave her alone until then.

JACKIE. Seriously?

RICARDO. Sonia is one of the most complicated people I've ever met. She has opposite's disease, she'll say she wants something cold but she really means she wanted it hot and you're just supposed to know that.

JACKIE. Are you guys happy? Is your sex life okay?

RICARDO. Jackie!

JACKIE. You needa start talking, Dad, what you're doing obviously isn't working for you...

(**RICARDO**'s *phone sounds. He gets a text, he reads it as he speaks.*)

JACKIE. Is that MOM??

RICARDO. No it's Alejandro...*(reads text)* I think Penelope is going through some heavy stuff right now.

JACKIE. Well ya, she kinda fucked up her shit.

RICARDO. Poor guy, maybe we should go over there and cheer him...THEM, up.

(RICARDO *types a text.*)

JACKIE. Is there someone else, Dad?

RICARDO. Oh, yum he's making flautas! Let's surprise them! I can pick up some sangria on the way over.

(JACKIE *stares at* RICARDO *as types a text.*)

JACKIE. Sand. Fucking Sand.

RICARDO. What was that?

JACKIE. Nothing, I'm starving

(JACKIE *gets up to leave.* RICARDO *is still playing with his phone.* JACKIE *rolls her eyes and walks off stage.*)

RICARDO. You know my Mom used to make the best... (*notices he is alone*) Jackie?

(*Lights out.*)

THE LETTER

(SONIA sits at a desk and writes, she reads aloud.)

SONIA. Dear Jackie,

If you're reading this – …No that's stupid. Stupid, Stupid.

(SONIA scribbles out the words and begins again.)

Dearest Jackie,

I wanted to write you and explain some things – …Well obviously Sonia, idiot *(slaps her head)* think, think…

Jackie,

I've loved you for oceans, but I can't really swim. Sadness gets in my nose and then my mouth tastes like a wet mop. We never really talked about the last time I left, well when I was in the hospital. It's a sensitive subject, but know that I was sick that time. That said, I want you to know that my sickness has nothing to do with you. I left this time because…

The reason I had to go was…

Well, simple really…it was a question of asphyxiation. See Jackie, I was never prepared to be a mother or a leader of two people. I was barely given the training to be a functioning human being…I've been faking it, because if I treated you like my mother did you'd be addicted to Zoloft too and well that's not fun and super expensive.

I left because I can't breathe, honey. I just needed some air. Simple as that.

I love you,

Mom.

(SONIA re-reads the letter. Then crumbles it up and throws it across the stage.)

(Lights out.)

BABY MAMA DRAMA

*(Kitchen, **ALEJANDRO** wears rubber gloves and intensely cleans the sink. A knock at the door, **ALEJANDRO** doesn't hear it. **RICARDO** invites himself in.)*

*(**RICARDO** watches **ALEJANDRO** scrub for a moment, he grins at **ALEJANDRO**'s neurotic attempt to release tension.)*

RICARDO.	ALEJANDRO.
You missed/ a spot.	HOLY SHIT.

RICARDO. I'm sorry, the door was open.

ALEJANDRO. Ya I leave it open when I'm cooking.

RICARDO. OH, why did I scare you so much then?

ALEJANDRO. You just have that affect on me.

*(**ALEJANDRO** continues to clean the counter. **RICARDO** watches.)*

RICARDO. I'm guessing it didn't go so well, I brought some sangria to cheer you up.

ALEJANDRO. What makes you say that? *(scrubs harder)* I mean, I made delicious foods.
You have a lesbian child and I have a pregnant child. AND Sonia is having a gay old time on VACATION!

*(**ALEJANDRO** throws his sponge in the sink and checks the oven.)*

ALEJANDRO. Are you stoned? Addicted to tranquilizers? Why THE FUCK, are you always so calm.

RICARDO. I dunno, you have that affect on me.

*(**ALEJANDRO** makes eye contact with **RICARDO** for the first time.)*

ALEJANDRO. You want ass?
How could you want ass at a time like this? My daughter is pregnant! It's hard enough supporting the two of us, How am I gonna manage another mouth to feed.

RICARDO. She's gonna keep it?

ALEJANDRO. Oh God, of course she is Ricardo. Why are you even here? Why are YOU HERE?..What Do you WANT?

RICARDO. Me and Jackie wanted to cheer you guys up. We brought Sangria/

*(**ALEJANDRO** snatches the bottle of Sangria out of **RICARDO**'s hand and inspects the bottle.)*

ALEJANDRO. Well THANKFULLY I made extra food.

RICARDO. It smells amazing.

ALEJANDRO. Of course it does, flautas are Penelope's favorite. OH SHIT, the beans/

*(A moment. **ALEJANDRO** stirs a pot.)*

*(**JACKIE** and **PENELOPE** enter, **PENELOPE** is playing with her belly.)*

PENELOPE. Dude, I don't want to get fat.

JACKIE. Don't eat so much then.

ALEJANDRO. Honey, you're eating for two now…you have to eat more.

PENELOPE. Ugh.

ALEJANDRO. We have company, please set the table girls.

PENELOPE. I can't/

ALEJANDRO. Why is that?

PENELOPE. I'm pregnant, I'm not supposed to be on my feet.

ALEJANDRO. GRRRR.

*(**ALEJANDRO** throws the dish rag across the room.)*

*(**JACKIE** grabs **PENELOPE**'s hand.)*

JACKIE. I'll help you dude. Come on.

*(**JACKIE** and **PENELOPE** walk to the pantry closet on the other side of the stage and take out plates.)*

*(**RICARDO** picks up the dish rag and brings it to **ALEJANDRO**, who stirs the beans like a mad man.)*

ALEJANDRO. Do you want something to drink?

RICARDO. I'm fine thanks. Are you okay?

(RICARDO *puts the dish rag on* ALEJANDRO*'s shoulder.* ALEJANDRO *continues to cook without making eye contact.*)

ALEJANDRO. I'm fucking great..I have some guacamole if you want to munch on something.

RICARDO. *(whispers)* I need to talk to you.

(ALEJANDRO *self consciously looks to* PENELOPE *to see if she heard, He raises his voice as he speaks.*)

ALEJANDRO. *(loudly towards the girls)* Or a beer? Corona, Pacifico, I can make you a michelada if you want.

(RICARDO *looks to* JACKIE, JACKIE *pretends not to notice them as she counts napkins.*)

RICARDO. *(whispers)* Can we go in the other room for a second.

ALEJANDRO. *(whispers aggressively)* NO, Jesus.

RICARDO. *(whispers)* Look I just need a moment alone with you/

ALEJANDRO. You're shit outta luck.

RICARDO. Asshole!

(JACKIE *and* PENELOPE *stop for a moment and look to their Dads.*)

JACKIE. Everything okay?

RICARDO. Fine. Great.

(PENELOPE *shrugs and goes to set the table,* JACKIE *follows reluctantly.*)

RICARDO. *(whispers)* I really need to talk/

ALEJANDRO. *(in normal voice)* You're just hungry. It's almost ready.

RICARDO. No that's not it.

ALEJANDRO. Maybe you just need to go out and get a massage, I can drop Jackie off after dinner.

JACKIE. Dad do you want me to get you some Advil.

RICARDO. No thanks. *(whispers)* I think I need you.

ALEJANDRO. He's okay Jackie, it's probably just all that stress. I think you need a bath.

A nice hot bath to release all that tension you keep in your shoulders.

RICARDO. No that's not it.

JACKIE. Well what is it Dad?

PENELOPE. Maybe you need ice cream Mr. Martinez?

ALEJANDRO. OR tea? I can warm some tea for you/

(**RICARDO** *walks to* **ALEJANDRO** *who is not making eye contact, rather cooking and pacing around the kitchen.*)

RICARDO. Look at me.

ALEJANDRO. I can't right now I'm cooking the beans.

RICARDO. You're terrified of me.

ALEJANDRO. No, Ricardo I don't want the beans to burn.

(**RICARDO** *gets even closer to* **ALEJANDRO**. **ALEJANDRO** *stirs the beans and avoids eye contact.*)

(**JACKIE** *and* **PENELOPE** *stop setting the table and watch.*)

JACKIE. Dad, I don't think he wants to talk to you/

RICARDO. I just want you in the most simple way possible/

ALEJANDRO. Damn, the beans need some more salt.

RICARDO. Alejandro, just look over here and talk to me/

(**ALEJANDRO** *snaps and lunges at* **RICARDO**.)

(*A surprised* **RICARDO** *is cornered,* **ALEJANDRO** *gets in his face and puts his hands around* **RICARDO***'s throat.*)

ALEJANDRO. WHAT DO YOU WANT FROM ME-

RICARDO. Stop.

(**RICARDO** *shoves* **ALEJANDRO** *Off of him.* **ALEJANDRO** *retaliates and pushes* **RICARDO** *into the wall.*)

ALEJANDRO. WHAT? YOU FAGGOT!

(ALEJANDRO punches RICARDO in the face.)

ALEJANDRO. YOU WANT A WAY OUT AND I'M NOT YOUR WAY!

(RICARDO gets away from ALEJANDRO and to the other side of the kitchen. He covers his face.)

(ALEJANDRO grows self conscious now that he notices the girls. He quickly goes back to cooking.)

ALEJANDRO. Dinner's ready.

(PENELOPE stands nervously.)

(JACKIE runs to RICARDO to make sure he is okay.)

(ALEJANDRO goes back to cooking, this time he stir the beans like a crack head.)

JACKIE. What the fuck was THAT?

ALEJANDRO. What do you mean?

(ALEJANDRO takes a taste of the beans.)

ALEJANDRO. MMM, just right.

JACKIE. Uh, hello?

You were about to kick my Dad's ass.

RICARDO. Hey, Jackie/

JACKIE. Dude Dad, come on. You look tore up.

RICARDO. It's been a long day.

ALEJANDRO. FUCK YES.

JACKIE. Well Mom's not here so, we need to resolve shit on our own.

PENELOPE. Dude Jackie, I don't think they wanna talk about it. Maybe we should just eat.

ALEJANDRO. What is it with this Sonia fascination? I mean, she JUST drives the carpool.

PENELOPE. You're so in denial.

JACKIE. No dude, he's jealous.

ALEJANDRO. Of what Jackie?

JACKIE. My mom. You wish people needed you like that, don't you?

ALEJANDRO. Ricardo, are you gonna control your daughter?

JACKIE. You can talk to ME. My Dad isn't my keeper.

RICARDO. Jackie, you need to breathe/

JACKIE. I know what's up, you guys. I'm not stupid.

PENELOPE. *(whispers)* Dude are you high? Let's just eat the stupid flautas and drop it.

JACKIE. Dad?

RICARDO. Jackie we're guests we shouldn't talk to our host that way.

PENELOPE. *(whispers)* Dude you're totally gonna get it if you don't shut it!

JACKIE. Are you guys FUCKING?

PENELOPE. WHHAAAA?? DUUUUUDE!

(a beat)

ALEJANDRO. Excuse me?

JACKIE. Are you guys fucking?? Dad? Come on don't lie to me, NOT to my face.

*(No response. **ALEJANDRO** and **RICARDO** make nervous eye contact.)*

JACKIE. ANSWER the question you guys.

PENELOPE. Dad?

ALEJANDRO. Ricardo, can you help out here?

PENELOPE. Dude, that explains why my Dad has been locking the doors around the house lately.

JACKIE. YA and why my dad gets all emotional in the garage late at night.

RICARDO. Jackie/

PENELOPE. Is that why Sonia left?

RICARDO. No, no. Guys/

JACKIE. No dude, but she totally knew about it.

RICARDO. What? No way.

ALEJANDRO. No, Jackie I think YOU are high.

JACKIE. You guys are soooo obvious, both of you. It's like you WANTED to get caught.

RICARDO. WHAT, no Jackie/

ALEJANDRO. PSH, Sonia's so deep in her own sorrow, she wouldn't notice if a bomb went off in her own uterus.

JACKIE. No, she knew, totally. She didn't care though, cuz once she told me you guys got married cuz of me anyways.

RICARDO. Jackie, that's not something you talk about in front of people.

JACKIE. Ya well you're not supposed to hit each other either. Can't we like call the cops on him or something???

ALEJANDRO. Ricardo? Are you gonna be proactive here? Or just sit and sulk.

(**RICARDO** *angrily looks to* **ALEJANDRO**.)

RICARDO. No Jackie. Mr. Lopez and I are not having sex.

(**RICARDO** *politely gets up and fixes the collar on his shirt.*)

RICARDO. Come on, Jackie lets get going. Thank Mr. Lopez for dinner. *(to Alejandro)* Thanks for the, perspective. Alejandro. I'll see myself to the door.

(**RICARDO** *exits,* **JACKIE** *quickly follows.*)

(**ALEJANDRO** *watches them leave.*)

(*He looks to* **PENELOPE** *who hands him his spoon for the beans.*)

(**ALEJANDRO** *takes the spoon. He stirs the beans and nods to himself.*)

(**PENELOPE** *goes back to setting the table.*)

(*Lights out.*)

CABO WABO

SONIA. Our honeymoon was a sign, or at least that's what I tell myself to justify one of the worst trips of my LIFE. Ricardo and I went to Cabo San Lucas, also known as the uncircumcised gringo tip of Baja California Mexico. As soon as we got off the plane, it was utter disaster like with yellow caution tape. I got the shits, first of all, which was not attractive and did not lead to sex which is the point of a honeymoon. Then Ricardo got a sun burn, that was well disgusting. His skin got all bubbly and oozy, and my squeamish tendencies only made him self conscious and pissy at ME. And THEN a hurricane hit, for three days. We were imprisoned on separate sides of the hotel room, being grossed out at each other's ailments while trying to recuperate, together, yet completely alone. Then, alleluia, Sunlight! No poopiness, sunburn gone. Finally, a day to enjoy Cabo and a day to enjoy each other. We took a boat to the middle island which divides two oceans, the Pacific and Sea of Cortez. The captain of the water taxi: a topless questionably drunk Mexican fisherman, told us to visit Divorce Beach which was literally just the other side of the island. Ricardo wanted to tan, so he stuck to the front beach the while I, out of sheer curiosity, ventured island. As I walked, the cocaine white sand burnt my toes and a trail of feet lead me to the most violent piece of ocean I had ever seen, or Divorce Beach. Each wave was bigger than the last, with a HUGE SPLASH of sea on the sand, that made you wonder if the water was coming from the sky or the ground. I swear, the water called to me, and I mean no one dare swim on Divorce beach, but I kept walking and walking...to hear "SONIAAA, SONIAAA" as the break unfolded in front of my sedated body. A shrieking voice took me out of it. I turned to find Ricardo running from a distance screaming for me to come back to the safer part of the beach. I looked to him and I looked back into the abusive waves that punched the sand maliciously, and I considered walking into the ocean, rather than be saved by my husband. On that particular day, I felt more of a connection with the waves than with my family.

(Lights out.)

BUENOS NACHOS

*(Later that night. **RICARDO**, still fully dressed, is asleep on the couch in front of a television.)*

*(**SONIA** enters looking together for the first time in the play, in a while. At first she confidently approaches **RICARDO** but quickly regrets it and steps back towards the door. She stands timidly as a FART sound is heard.)*

SONIA. ...Fucking chimichangas, ugh.

*(**RICARDO** rolls around on the couch for a moment but goes continues to sleep. **SONIA** shakes off her failed attempt and begins to approach **RICARDO** again, this time without any reservations BUT another strong fart sound is heard.)*

*(**RICARDO** wakes up this time.)*

RICARDO. Sonia? Sonia.

SONIA. My life has been full of things that give me an equal amount of pleasure and humiliation.

RICARDO. Mine too. Mine, too.

*(**SONIA** sits on the edge of the couch.)*

(Lights out.)

GOO, GOO LADY GAGA

(A bus stop, three months later. **PENELOPE** *has her ipod on and shakes her boobs to some music.* **JACKIE** *approaches timidly, she doesn't want to be seen by* **PENELOPE**. *They finally catch eyes, it's mad awkward.)*

PENELOPE. Oh hey.

JACKIE. Sup?

PENELOPE. Chillin. You?

JACKIE. Going to school. Aren't you?

PENELOPE. *(Sarcastic)* No, I'm going to China dude.

JACKIE. Bitchy much?

PENELOPE. Where's your mom? I thought she was just taking YOU to school from now on.

JACKIE. She had a doctors appointment today, so...

(Awkward silence.)

JACKIE. You listening to the new Lady Gaga?

PENELOPE. Ugh, of course.
I already know the first five songs by heart and the back up choreograph for the video.

JACKIE. No doubt.

(Awkward Silence.)

PENELOPE. Is Sonia sick or something?

JACKIE. No, my mom's going to a new therapist with my Dad.

PENELOPE. Word?

JACKIE. Ya, they're all about fixing shit right now. They even renewed their wedding vows and went to Cabo San Lucas for their second honeymoon.

PENELOPE. Hm, heard it's beautiful down there.

(Awkward Silence.)

JACKIE. You allowed to talk to me yet?

PENELOPE. Nope. You?

JACKIE. Nah, my Dad said never again.

PENELOPE. I never thought I would say this but I kinda miss the carpool and even...

PENELOPE.	**JACKIE.**
Juan Gabriel.	Juan Gabriel.

(They giggle.)

JACKIE. Dude, I've kinda been dying to tell you something/

PENELOPE. I don't wanna talk about our Dad's okay? It's really really weird to think about.

JACKIE. No, No...it's like on the personal growth tip.

PENELOPE. Oooooh. Did you finally start growing out your arm pit hair?

JACKIE. No fool.

I...kinda...got some, like booty or, uh, vag. I mean.

PENELOPE. No way. With WHO?

JACKIE. Marta finally came around.

PENELOPE. Ohhhhhh snap. What I say? What. Did. I. Say.

JACKIE. Dude, it was so dope.

PENELOPE. Really, dude?

JACKIE. She said I was A NATURAL. I like, have a new outlook on life and shit, it's trippy.

PENELOPE. Word. Be careful now, though, dude. In my experience sex is like a taco truck? Or was it a motorcycle?...

(PENELOPE *grabs her belly self consciously.)*

JACKIE. Is it a boy or a girl?

PENELOPE. Girl.

JACKIE. Awww, see you always wanted a little sister.

PENELOPE. Except she's my daughter stupid.

JACKIE. I know that/

PENELOPE. Well, what the fuck dude? It's way different. DUH.

JACKIE. Jeez, chillax.

PENELOPE. Sorry, I get all hormonal lately. Like the other day cried my eyes out while watching Gossip Girl/

JACKIE. Well it was an intense episode/

PENELOPE. No dude, I tore apart like a vanilla wafer, and I can never get enough desert nowadays either.

JACKIE. Word. Well maybe we can get ice cream after school today. I'll tell my Mom I missed the bus.

PENELOPE. Hm, that might be sick. I can tell my Dad that I'm going to Babies' R Us.

JACKIE. You know what you wanna name her?

PENELOPE. Ya, I'm thinking I want her to be named after some like really fierce woman from history.

JACKIE. Like who?

PENELOPE. Well, My list includes: Rihanna, Frida Kahlo, Lil' Kim, OR Sonia.

JACKIE. Wait, Sonia like after/my?

PENELOPE. The bus is here, dude.

(**JACKIE** *and* **PENELOPE** *walk off stage together.*)

(Lights out.)

End of Play